# Nikki & Deja

# Birthday Blues

by Karen English

Illustrated by Laura Freeman

Clarion Books ★ New York

To all the Nikkis and Dejas everywhere
—K.E.

To my sister, Roberta
—L.F.

Clarion Books
an imprint of Houghton Mifflin Harcourt Publishing Company
215 Park Avenue South, New York, NY 10003
Text copyright © 2009 by Karen English
Illustrations copyright © 2009 by Laura Freeman

The illustrations were executed digitally.
The text was set in 13.5-point Warnock Pro.

www.clarionbooks.com

Printed in the U.S.A.

*Library of Congress Cataloging-in-Publication Data*
English, Karen.
Nikki and Deja : birthday blues / by Karen English ; illustrated by Laura Freeman.
p. cm.
Summary: As her eighth birthday approaches, Deja's biggest concern is whether
her father will attend her party, until her aunt is called away on business and
a classmate schedules a "just because party" on the same afternoon.
ISBN 978-0-618-97787-1
[1. Birthdays—Fiction. 2. Parties—Fiction. 3. Schools—Fiction. 4. Best friends—
Fiction. 5. Friendship—Fiction. 6. Aunts—Fiction.] I. Freeman-Hines, Laura, ill.
II. Title.
PZ7.E7232Nik 2009
[Fic]—dc22    2007050189

WOZ  10  9  8  7  6  5  4  3  2  1

# – Contents –

# 1

# The Way to Clean a Bedroom

"It's my birthday, it's my birthday, it's my birthday..." Deja makes a chant out of "It's my birthday" and dances to the beat of it around Nikki's backyard. It is a bright and shining Saturday morning, the best day of the week.

"It's not your birthday," Nikki reminds her.

"But it will be in seven more days, and I'm going to be eight way before you." Deja stops her made-up dance so she can think about the next thing more clearly. She doesn't want to say it out loud, so she says it in her head. *And this time my daddy might come for my birthday.* She looks up at the sky in search of a sign, then recites a little prayer. She glances over at Nikki sitting on the back porch, wondering if she can read her thoughts.

"I'm getting heelies, boots, and a bright pink T-shirt with my name in rhinestones. I already saw it at Twizzles' Fashions for Tweens." Deja stops again to imagine herself wearing it.

"With 'Deja' on it?" Nikki asks.

"I can get it put on," Deja says with confidence, even though she doesn't know where or how. Maybe her daddy will come, and maybe he'll give her a hundred dollars to buy whatever she wants. "Write this down, Nikki."

Nikki takes out her pad, removes the kitty cap from her special pen, and waits.

"We're having games first, then the playoffs with the winners. Auntie Dee's getting a huge stuffed panda bear as a prize. Then we'll have a dance contest—with me as the judge—then pizza and punch, and then ice cream and cake . . ." Deja takes a breath. "Then everyone will watch me open my presents. Then we'll watch *Mouse Queen Takes Hollywood,* which I know I'm getting for my birthday, too."

"How do you know?" Nikki asks.

"I kinda really think I am," Deja says, as if that is that.

Deja looks down at the citrine ring that she got on her last birthday. Auntie Dee had promised she'd buy Deja a birthstone ring if she could keep from biting her nails for a month.

Every morning at breakfast, Auntie Dee had said to Deja, "Show me whatcha got." Deja would hold out her hands, palms down, to prove she hadn't bitten her nails during the night. She'd really wanted that citrine ring with the fourteen-carat gold band. She'd especially liked the feel of the word coming out of her mouth: "citrine." Maybe when she grew up and had a husband and a little girl, she'd name her Citrine.

Nikki had said it was stupid to name a baby after a ring.

"What about Dyamond Taylor in Mr. Beaumont's room?" Deja had said. "She's named after a diamond, only it's spelled different."

Deja thinks about Griselda Castilla, who sits in her row at school. She was the first to have a citrine ring. It glinted in the light every time Griselda moved her pencil across her paper. But Deja wasn't trying to copy Griselda. She can't help it if her birthstone is a citrine, too.

"How do you know you're getting heelies?" Nikki says.

"'Cause." Deja sits down next to Nikki and slips her thumb into her mouth. The citrine ring in its gold setting sparkles on her index finger.

"Can I wear your ring?" Nikki asks.

Deja pretends she doesn't hear her.

"Come on, let me wear it for a day."

Deja doesn't say anything on purpose. She thinks of her messy room. She could probably get Nikki to help her clean it. Auntie Dee told her that she needed to clean her room before going outside—yet she hasn't done it. She'd known she wasn't going to. When Auntie said it, Deja thought immediately of how she would put it off. She did that sometimes.

Now Auntie Dee is across the street at her friend Phoebe's, sorting a bunch of stuff for a garage sale that's coming up. She'll be back soon, and then Deja will get in trouble. Probably get

put on punishment. Maybe Auntie Dee will even cancel Deja's upcoming birthday party.

"I'll let you wear it . . . on one condition."

Nikki looks at Deja suspiciously. "What?"

"You have to help me clean my room."

"That's not fair. Your room is too messy."

"You want to wear my ring or not?" Deja holds up her hand in front of Nikki's face with her fingers spread, then wiggles them back and forth like a beauty queen.

Nikki purses her lips. "Okay. Come on, let's get it over with."

Deja looks away and smiles.


"Where does this go?" Nikki holds up a pink pajama bottom. Deja stares at it for a moment, squinting.

"Put it under the bed."

"Under the bed?"

"I have too many things on the hooks already."

"It can go in the dirty clothes."

"It's not dirty enough."

"What about in your dresser drawer?"

"Just put it under the bed. It's not clean enough for my drawer."

Nikki shrugs and pushes the pajama bottom

under the bed. Then she gets down on her hands and knees and looks. "There's a whole lot of stuff under here. And Bear! How come you don't play with Bear anymore?" Nikki pulls Bear out and leans him against Deja's nightstand.

"I do play with Bear. I just forgot where he was," Deja says.

Nikki pulls out a blue sweater, a Monopoly set, a purple mitten, some crumpled scribbled-on notebook paper, broken crayons, an apple core. "Deja, look at all this stuff! I change my mind. Your room is yucky." She flops down on the bed and sticks out her lip.

"Come on, you have to help me! Auntie Dee told me to clean my room, and she's gonna come back soon, and then I'm gonna get in trouble."

"You shoulda done what she told you."

"Plus, if I get in trouble, you'll have to go home, and then we won't get to work on our map."

This seems to catch Nikki's attention. She looks up at the corner of the ceiling, thinking.

Deja waits. They're studying maps in Social Studies, and Ms. Shelby has given the class an assignment to create a neighborhood map. She said that they could work with a partner.

Deja got excited right away. She started making plans. She and Nikki would be partners, of course. They would start their map on Saturday, and they would include every house and also Global Tire and Brakes, the re-sell shop and Babe's Barbecue—*everything*. Their map was going to be the best one of all.

"Okay, okay." Nikki gets up and looks around at the mess on the floor: socks, barrettes, pennies, wire coat hangers, playing cards. Slowly, she begins to pick up the cards. She plucks pennies and paper clips from the carpet and drops them into a paper cup that is on the floor as well. She sighs. "You have to clean under your bed. *I'm* not cleaning there."

"Yeah, yeah . . ." Deja thinks of Nikki's room. In Nikki's room, everything has a place, and there is a place for everything. Nikki never has to search for her other mitten or her muffler or the mate to her flip-flop.

Just then the front door slams. They both stop to listen. It's Auntie! She'll be coming upstairs any minute.

"Auntie Dee's back!" Deja says, hurrying around the room, stuffing various articles into drawers and under the bed. She throws an old backpack covered with ink stains and dark smudges to Nikki to shove into the closet.

Auntie Dee's footsteps sound on the stairs.

Deja pulls up the sheet and blanket on her bed, then yanks the comforter into place. She grabs the pillows off the floor and props them against the headboard. When Auntie Dee walks into the room, Deja and Nikki are sitting on the bed side by side with their hands in their laps. Auntie Dee stops in the doorway. "What?"

"Nothing," Deja says.

"Then why are you sitting there like that?" Auntie Dee looks around the room and squints. "Mmm," she says. "Dare I check under the bed?"

Deja keeps her mouth closed.

Auntie Dee chuckles to herself. She moves out of the doorway and goes back down the hall.

"Can we go to the store?" Deja calls out while scrambling off the bed. She picks up Bear and pulls Nikki after her. They hurry out of the room.

"As a matter of fact, we do need milk," Auntie Dee answers. She digs around in her purse and pulls out her wallet. "Here's some money. Make sure you bring me back the right change."

"Okay," Deja says. She grabs Nikki's hand and they start down the hall.

Out on the porch, Deja sets Bear on the swing. Just before they skip down the front steps, Nikki stops and puts out her hand. "The ring," she says.

"You didn't really help me that much," says Deja.

"I did so. And you promised."

Reluctantly, Deja twists at her ring. "I don't know if I can get it off."

"You promised, Deja."

Deja pulls and twists, but the ring stays on her finger.

"Lick your finger."

Deja sucks her teeth, then licks her finger. With a little more tugging, the ring slides off. She rolls her eyes as she hands it over. Nikki takes the ring out of Deja's hand with the hem of her T-shirt and proceeds to rub the leftover spit off it. She slips it on her ring finger, then holds up her hand.

"You've got to give it back to me on Monday."

Nikki doesn't seem to hear. She wiggles her fingers slowly to make the ring sparkle.

"Monday, Nikki," Deja insists.

"Okay. I already heard you."

Nikki is looking at Deja's citrine ring as if it is now hers. Deja wants to snatch it back, but it is firmly on Nikki's finger.

# 2

# Mapping the Neighborhood

$M$r. Delvecchio is sitting on a stool behind the counter reading the newspaper. He says he reads the entire paper every day. He'll tell you that every time you go into his store. "Helps the day pass during the slow times," he says before he lowers it to peer at Deja and Nikki. Occasionally Mr. Delvecchio comes from the other side of the counter to straighten the canned goods on the shelf. Deja suspects he might be checking to make sure they don't take anything. That doesn't feel too good, but she likes Mr. D. anyway. Some kids do take things, so that makes him be on guard.

"I think somebody's got a birthday comin' up soon," he says, surprising her. That's the funny thing about Mr. Delvecchio. One minute he's stern, and the next his eyes are crinkling with a smile and he's saying something nice.

Deja remembers telling him about her birthday last week. She always starts trumpeting her birthday early, so everyone knows it's coming.

"What are the big plans?" he asks with a twinkle in his eye.

"I'm having a game party—where we're going to play all kinds of games."

"Mmm. That's a first for me," he says before going back to his paper.

Nikki moves away to check the candy display, and Deja goes to the back of the store to the refrigerated case for a half-gallon of milk.

Out on the street, Deja walks backward. "Mr. Delvecchio remembered I have a birthday coming up."

"Who doesn't?" Nikki says.

"Maybe he's going to get me something. Maybe he's going to let me have free candy."

Nikki rolls her eyes and holds out her bag of hot chips. Deja reaches in and plucks a few out. "Let's go the long way back," she says. That would be down Maynard to Ashby, the street past Fulton, a left turn down Ashby, another left on

Marin, and back to Fulton. "Then we can remember what to put on our map."

They pass Rick B's Junkyard, with its deadly looking fence topped with coiled razor wire. They always look straight ahead while tiptoeing by, hoping not to alert Prince, Rick B's ferocious and fearsome rottweiler. He is too horrible to even glance at, even though a chainlink fence separates them from him.

"Where you think Prince is?" Deja says in a near whisper.

"I don't care about Prince," Nikki says, but she looks over her shoulder and quickens her step. Once they are safely past the junkyard, she turns around and cups her mouth. "Hey, Prince! You ugly ol' dog," she calls out. "Who's afraid of you?"

They wait to see him charge the fence, barking and snarling and racing back and forth. But this time Prince doesn't make an appearance. *Must be sleeping,* Deja thinks.

They pass Perfect Beauty Hair Salon and Nail Emporium on Ashby. They peer in the window and see Mrs. Broadie, the cafeteria lady, getting her hair done. One side of her hair sticks out all over, and one side is slick to her head. They look at each other and burst into laughter. "She looks funny," Nikki says.

"Don't let her see you," Deja says, pulling Nikki after her. Mrs. Broadie can be mean, especially if you take an extra pudding or miss picking up the small bowl of green beans. "Get those beans," she'll say.

"Write this down, Nikki," Deja says.

Nikki pulls out her notebook from the pouch she wears around her neck.

"On our map we're also going to have Babe's Barbecue, Global Tire and Brakes, and Your History Bookstore."

Nikki writes quickly, then looks up.

"And Perfect Beauty Hair Salon and Nail Emporium . . ." Deja squints, thinking. "Oh, and Puerto Nuevo Restaurant."

"Wait, hold on. I can't write that fast."

When Nikki finally lifts her pen from her pad, Deja continues a little more slowly. "Rick B's Junkyard."

"I don't want that on our map," Nikki says.

"How come?"

"'Cause he's got that ugly dog."

"Prince can't hurt you just because we put the junkyard on our map."

"I know that," Nikki says. Then, in a quieter voice, she adds, "I just don't want to be reminded of him."

Deja knows that Nikki is afraid of dogs. If she sees one at the end of the block, she'll cross the street or go the other way. She doesn't even like to go to someone's house where there's a dog. She can walk by the junkyard only because Prince is always behind a fence. Deja doesn't say anything, but she plans to include the junkyard. It takes up half a block. It would be too hard to leave it out.

They walk on at a slower pace. Deja shifts the half-gallon of milk in her arms. "Anyway, Auntie Dee says dogs are more afraid of us than we are of them."

Nikki presses her lips together as if the notion makes her a little suspicious. "I don't believe it," she says.

After a while Deja says, "Don't forget Simply Delicious Health Food Store." She points to the other side of the street. It is Auntie Dee's favorite neighborhood store. Deja suspects it is because of the owner. Auntie Dee always seems flustered and gushy whenever he is at the register, and Deja doesn't like that. She never says anything, but it annoys her to see Auntie Dee acting so silly. She can't put into words just what it is that bothers her, though.

❀

Back at home, Auntie Dee has bought them a bright yellow poster board for their map. They take all of their supplies out to Deja's front porch. Nikki carries the markers and rulers, and Deja brings the poster board and pencils. There they begin to work on different sections, in pencil first. Deja draws the lines for their street in the middle. Then they begin working on the streets around Fulton. At one point, Auntie Dee steps around them to go to her car in the driveway. "Good job," she says. Nikki is working on writing "Perfect Beauty Hair Salon and Nail Emporium" as neatly as possible, and Deja is coloring in trees and bushes.

Deja sits back to admire her work. She can't help but smile. She thinks of Monday morning, when everyone will bring in their neighborhood maps. She thinks of all the kids gathered around her and Nikki's map—and of the oohs and aahs and the secret disappointments about their own less beautiful maps. She pictures the maps on the thin newsprint that Ms. Shelby passed out to those who said they wouldn't be able to get poster board. She smiles, thinking about how great theirs will look in comparison.

Just then Nikki and Deja hear a low rumble. It grows louder, and they look up in time to see

Antonia skating past. As she glides by, she squats down into a sitting position, then turns to look at Deja, without expression. Immediately, she's standing up again, skating off down the street. Nikki and Deja stare at her.

"Why'd she give me that mean look?" Deja asks.

"She didn't give you a mean look," Nikki says.

"She did, too."

"Maybe she knows about your birthday party. Maybe she's mad 'cause she's not invited."

"But she *is* invited. Auntie's making me." Deja purses her lips together. "Showoff. I can do that!" she says, though she just learned to skate two months before.

Nikki quietly goes back to their map. Deja begins working on the pond at Miller's Park. Miller's Park is where she had her last birthday party. She liked it because the pond has ducks. She remembers feeding those ducks with her daddy there a long time ago.

# 3

# Presentations

"You can carry the map to Marburn, then I can carry it the rest of the way to school," Deja says as Nikki comes down her porch steps on Monday with their map rolled up and held by a rubber band.

"Why do you get to carry it to school?"

"'Cause you got to have it last night."

"But I kept it rolled up."

"Come on, Nikki. It's almost my birthday. Plus I was the one who made sure we had a map key and a compass rose."

"It's been almost your birthday for the last two weeks. And I was the one who remembered the map scale."

Deja ignores this. "When it's almost your birthday, you keep saying it, too."

"Not like you."

Deja thinks about this. Then she remembers her ring. "It's time to give back my ring, anyway."

Nikki looks at her hand as if she's forgotten that Deja's ring is on her finger. She sighs, licks her finger, and slips it off.

Antonia and her daddy drive by just as Nikki and Deja turn the corner to Carver Elementary. Dyamond and Ayanna race over.

"Dyamond wants to know if she can come to your birthday party," Ayanna says right in front of Dyamond. Auntie Dee had said Deja could invite every girl in her class, but she didn't say anything about the girls in Mr. Beaumont's class.

"I have to ask," Deja says.

Dyamond shows her extra-big permanent teeth in a kind of half smile.

Deja watches Antonia's car pull up to the curb in front of the school. Her dad gets out, goes around the car, and opens the door for Antonia. Then they both go to the back of the car. He pops the trunk.

"Come on, Nikki. Let's get to the line." Suddenly, Deja is anxious to show off her and Nikki's creation. She can just hear everyone's "Wow"s.

"Put your projects on the round table," Ms. Shelby says to the entering students. Several have big poster boards, but none are as colorful as Nikki and Deja's. A few have the newsprint paper Ms. Shelby had passed out. The usual knuckleheads come in empty-handed. They have excuses, though. Ms. Shelby just holds up her palm. "Save your excuses. I'll know who hasn't turned in their map project soon enough."

The door opens, but no one comes in. It is Antonia, holding it open for her dad. It is hard for him to get through it with Antonia's enormous map in his arms. Ms. Shelby rushes in front of him to clear books and papers off the other round table. "You can put that here," she says.

Gently he lowers the map onto the table, then stands back, brushing his hands together. He gives Antonia a little wave and turns to leave.

"Wow," Carlos says, letting out a low whistle. A few children drift over to Antonia's map project, then several more follow. Soon most of the class is staring down at Antonia's spectacular three-dimensional neighborhood map. It has cardboard buildings, plastic trees, and the pond at Miller's Park is made out of slightly crumpled aqua-blue plastic wrap. "Wow,"

Carlos says again, and Deja wants to punch him.

Deja glances at their own map under the pile of nearly identical poster-board maps. She's mortified to discover nothing very special about her and Nikki's effort, after all.

Deja feels her mouth grow heavy. She has to concentrate on not letting it sag at the corners. She feels embarrassed. Then she feels angry. It isn't fair. She could tell by the way Antonia's dad stood back and looked down at the map that he was looking at his own handiwork. It isn't fair! Not even a little bit! Deja catches Nikki's eye and sees her looking just as unhappy.

Ms. Shelby joins the students at the table. "My," she says. "My, my." She doesn't say anything else. Antonia stands back with a satisfied smile. She looks over at the other map projects, and Deja thinks she sees Antonia's smile turn into a smirk. It isn't fair.

"Okay everyone," Ms. Shelby says. "Let's get to our seats. I'm so glad to see so many projects. Most of you have done such a great job."

Antonia's smile fades a bit. Deja knows she is wondering how Ms. Shelby could lump her project in with the rest. Hers is obviously the best one. Hers is in a class by itself.

"Antonia has the best map," Carlos says from his seat behind Deja's.

"Her daddy helped her," Deja says over her shoulder. "I bet you he did it all."

"You're just jealous," Carlos says calmly. Deja wants to punch him, again. She remembers that Carlos is always saying things that make her want to punch him. Like the time he teased her for sucking her thumb. They were watching a film about the disappearing rain forest, and she had simply forgotten she was at school. Before she knew it, Carlos was laughing out loud and pointing. Too late. She yanked her thumb out of her mouth, but not before several other kids saw her. "Deja sucks her thumb! Deja sucks her thumb," someone started chanting. It was a playground chant for days. Until finally kids forgot about it. Or maybe they just stored it away, and the least little thing could make them remember.

"Why should I be jealous of someone who can't even do her own map project?"

"You're just jealous," he says again.

Deja fumes.

It's okay," Deja says, referring to Antonia's project. Deja and Nikki are sitting at the lunch table, sharing Deja's celery sticks and peanut butter.

Nikki licks the peanut butter completely off hers. "Antonia's is better than ours."

"It's not better. It's different."

"It's better," Nikki repeats.

"Different," Deja says again. But somehow she doesn't sound convincing, even to her own ears.

# The Map of Many Clever Features

Map presentations begin after lunch, during Social Studies.

"Who wants to go first?" Ms. Shelby asks in her encouraging tone. She always sounds like a cheerleader when it is time for project presentations.

Deja's hand shoots up before Ms. Shelby even gets the question completely out. "We want to go first, Ms. Shelby," Deja says.

Nikki gives her a questioning look. Deja knows Nikki hates this part of a project—getting up in front of everyone to present it. But she ignores Nikki.

"Great!" Ms. Shelby says. She is probably happy that she doesn't have to "volunteer" anyone.

Deja retrieves their map from the round table and marches up to the front of the class. Nikki gets out of her seat slowly and follows, looking miserable.

"Nikki's going to hold the map, and I'm going to explain it." Deja hands the map to Nikki, who looks relieved. She won't have to talk.

"Nikki and I live next door to each other," Deja says, pointing to their two houses. "As you all know." She proceeds to point out Vianda's house across the street, and Keyon Denver's house (he plays football at the junior college) next door, and Auntie Dee's friend Phoebe's house, and Miss Ida's house and Mr. D's store on the corner of Maynard Street, where they buy their hot chips. She shows them the junkyard and Simply Delicious Health Food Store, Puerto Nuevo Restaurant, Sir Galahad Cleaners, and Perfect Beauty Hair Salon and Nail Emporium. (Deja especially likes the word "emporium." She likes that it's a word her whole class has probably never had the occasion to say. They probably don't even know what it means.) She and Nikki had put Antonia's house on their map because they'd included all the houses, but she doesn't mention it now.

When Deja pauses to take a breath, Ms.

YOUR HISTORY
BOOKSTORE

MARIN STREET

GLOBAL TIRE
AND BRAKES

MR.
BOHANNA

BABE'S
BBQ

MR.
ROBINSON

PERFECT
BEAUTY
HAIR SALON
AND NAIL
EMPORIUM

NIKKI

BOBBY

RE-SELL
SHOP

DEJA

VIANDA

FULTON STREET

KEYON
DENVER

DARNELL

MISS
IDA

PHOEBE

RICK B'S
JUNKYARD

ANTONIA

MR. D'S

Shelby steps forward. "My, Deja! You and Nikki live in a great neighborhood. But you need to wrap it up so we'll have time for a few more presentations."

Deja nods reluctantly. "Well, I just want to say that Nikki and me live in the best neighborhood on the best street in the whole wide world."

There is a moment of silence before everyone breaks into polite applause. Deja takes the map out of Nikki's hands and returns it to the table. They both go back to their seats.

"Who's next?" Ms. Shelby asks, clapping her hands together once.

Ralph and Carlos raise their hands and go to get their flimsy newsprint map off the table.

*It isn't even colored,* Deja notes. And the street lines haven't even been drawn with a ruler. It looks hastily made, with little care. How could they stand up there holding that half-done map? What is *wrong* with boys?

But stand up there they do. Carlos holds the map, and Ralph points out their two houses, around the corner from each other, and the scribbled park with a crooked rectangle for the basketball court, and a few squares with misspelled store names on Post Boulevard. He finishes up and waits for applause.

Ms. Shelby nods at the class, then begins clapping. Everyone follows suit, but not with much enthusiasm.

"We'll go next, Ms. Shelby," Antonia volunteers. She looks over at her new friend, Casey, who stands up.

"We're going to need a table to rest our map on, but we'll tilt it up so that everyone can see." Antonia flips her long braid over her shoulder, then looks directly at Deja.

Carefully, Casey and Antonia carry the map to the table that Ms. Shelby has moved to the front of the class. Casey angles it up, and Antonia goes to the whiteboard to get Ms. Shelby's pointer—without asking.

She points to her house, mentioning her trampoline in the backyard and that her house is a split-level. In fact, it is the *only* split-level house on Fulton. She points out Casey's house around the block. Then she skips over the rest of the nearby streets to the park. She takes her time then, pointing out the many clever features. The miniature park benches, the tiny rubber ducks, a layer of real sand glued around the pond. When she finishes, she looks up and waits for the applause.

After a moment of silence, Ralph starts it off

with whoops and loud clapping. One by one, other kids join the noise and hoopla until Ms. Shelby has to hold up her hand and put a finger to her lips.

"All right, all right. We acknowledge that Antonia and Casey did a super job, but let's keep it down so we don't disturb the class next door."

It takes some moments before the clapping dies away. Carlos seems to want to keep it going. Probably because of what Deja said about Antonia's father doing all the work.

During recess, Ms. Shelby hangs most of the maps on the wall over the bookshelves in the class library. Deja is happy to see her and Nikki's, almost in the center. But Casey and Antonia's map has a place all its own on the round library table. Books have been cleared from the table just to give it room.

Deja counts up the days. She only has to see Antonia's map for two and a half more weeks, and then Ms. Shelby will be handing everything back to be carted home. Deja can't wait for that day to come.

Deja is quiet all the way home. Nikki is a chatterbox, talking about everybody's maps and comparing them to theirs. Deja thinks about

Antonia's map and how her father carried it into the classroom for her. Deja wonders how it feels to have your daddy help you with a school project and then carry it into the classroom for you. She tries to picture it, but it's hard. She hasn't seen her daddy in a long time because, as Auntie Dee says, he lives far away.

# 5

# Staying at Miss Ida's

As soon as Deja walks through the door after school, she comes upon Auntie Dee rushing around in a frenzy. She has a pile of laundry in her arms and she's racing toward her bedroom.

On the bed is an open suitcase. Auntie Dee begins to throw items into it from the mound of clean clothes on her bed: pajamas, jeans, T-shirts. . . . She runs to the closet and yanks her good dress, the one she wears to dinners and things, off the hanger. She holds it up in front of her. "Oh, well," she says and tosses it in the suitcase.

Deja finally thinks to say, "Auntie, where are you going?"

"Oh, baby . . . I've got to go out of town for my job."

Deja doesn't know what to think. Auntie never has to go out of town for her job.

"Someone I work with who always goes on these trips is sick. They asked me."

"But . . . what about me?" Deja asks.

Auntie Dee stops her packing and turns toward Deja. "Sweetie, you're going to stay at Miss Ida's."

"Miss Ida's?" A thousand questions dance around in Deja's head. "Will I still be there for my birthday?"

"Your birthday? No." Auntie Dee laughs. "It's just for a few days. I'll be back in plenty of time for your birthday." She snaps her fingers. "Lotion!" She focuses on Deja again. "Look, Deja, give out your invitations at school tomorrow. How about that?"

That doesn't make it feel better. "Why can't I stay with Nikki?"

"Because Nikki's dad is under the weather, and her mom has her hands full with him."

Deja doesn't understand that. Why can't Nikki's daddy take care of himself? Why would a grownup have to be taken care of just for being "under the weather"?

"We wouldn't bother Nikki's dad. I could help Nikki's mom take care of him."

Auntie Dee looks as if her mind is on her trip. "Hmm?" She rummages in her toiletry bag. "Toothpaste," she says, going toward the bathroom.

"Auntie, I could help out."

"No, Deja. That won't work. Besides, you'll be good company for Miss Ida. She'll love having you."

Deja thinks about her visits to Miss Ida's with Auntie Dee. She thinks about the doilies under the lamps and the dish of hard candy that is actually old and soft on the coffee table. She's had a piece. Plus Miss Ida keeps her drapes drawn all the time. It is so dark in her living room, she has to turn on the lamp, even during the day. Deja feels a tiny bit frightened. She's not sure if she can stay at Miss Ida's.

"Why can't Miss Ida stay here?"

"Well, you know, Deja, sometimes old folks like to be around their own things. I wanted to make this favor she's doing for us as easy as possible."

Deja frowns. "When do I have to go?"

"Tonight. I'll take you over there before Phoebe takes me to the airport."

Deja feels her throat tighten. She pictures Auntie not getting back in time for her birthday party on Saturday. She pictures herself stuck at Miss Ida's . . . forever.

"There's my girl," Miss Ida says, throwing open her front door. "Ooh, we gonna have a ball." She scoops up Deja into a big squishy bear hug. Deja almost can't breathe.

Deja tries to smile, but she can only manage a tiny one.

"She's got her clothes, Miss Ida, and I packed her lunch for school tomorrow. I should be back by Friday afternoon."

"Take your time. We'll be fine." Miss Ida squeezes Deja's shoulder. Deja wishes she could be sure she'll be fine. Her birthday is just five days away. What if Auntie doesn't get back in time?

Auntie bends down and kisses Deja's forehead. "I'll be home before you know it." She turns to head down the steps. "Be good," she calls over her shoulder.

Deja feels a frown plastered across her face. She stands at the door and scowls at it even after Miss Ida closes it.

"Come on, darling. I bet you're hungry."

No, she isn't hungry. Not even a little bit.

"I'll take your things, and you go on in the kitchen and have a seat. I'll be there in a minute."

Deja walks down Miss Ida's long dark hallway toward the kitchen. Something smells funny. It hits her as soon as she enters the room and sees the table set with two place settings. She takes a whiff. It's a horrible smell. She just can't eat anything that has a smell like that. She hears Auntie Dee's voice in her head: *It's impolite to turn your nose up at someone's food. You must always try to eat a little bit, just so feelings won't be hurt.*

"Now, these are my favorite vegetables, Deja," Miss Ida says as she comes into the kitchen and goes to the stove. "You like turnips?" She dishes out a plate and places it in front of Deja. Deja looks down. Fried chicken (that's good), green beans, a piece of white bread (Auntie Dee never buys white bread), and a smelly blob of turnips with watery edges. Deja swallows hard.

Miss Ida sits down across from her. She bows her head, and Deja bows her head, too. Miss Ida says a quick blessing and Deja joins her with "Amen." She is grateful to have food, as Auntie Dee always reminds her, but it is hard to be grateful for the nasty stuff. How is she going to get it down? Will she have to eat it all?

While she is thinking, a loud ringing fills the room. Deja looks over at the old-fashioned telephone with the funny dial. She remembers the first time she visited Miss Ida's. She and Auntie Dee had come to bring chicken soup. Miss Ida had been sick. Miss Ida's funny-looking telephone had caught Deja's eye. It had a round thing on the front with holes in it. Miss Ida had to call her friend to cancel a dinner. Deja couldn't figure out how she was going to use that funny telephone. As she watched Miss Ida dial the number, she wondered what would happen if someone was in a hurry. It was the slowest dialing phone she'd ever seen.

Miss Ida gets up to answer it and, quickly, before Deja can stop herself, she is spooning half of her own turnips onto Miss Ida's plate. She mixes them around, then looks at them carefully. Miss Ida finishes up with her niece, who is calling just to say "Hey."

"That Lilly is a real doll. Always calling to check up on her old aunt."

Deja says nothing. Miss Ida takes her seat across from Deja, and Deja waits to see if Miss Ida is going to say anything about her turnips. She doesn't.

In fact, that's just what she dives into first: a heaping spoonful of mushy turnips.

Deja takes a tiny spoonful of what is left of the turnips on her plate. She holds it in her mouth. She can't bring herself to swallow. She tries to, but feels a gag rising at the same time. Quickly, she takes a sip of milk. That's what she'll do. She will get the nasty turnips down with a sip of milk after each bite. But she has to rest first. She can't just dive in. She has to wait. She takes a bite of fried chicken. That helps get the yucky turnip taste out of her mouth. When she has her courage up, she does the turnip-milk thing again. It could work. She just has to go slow.

"I knew I forgot something," Miss Ida says suddenly. "I put up some pickled beets last fall. Delicious. I meant to dish you out some. But you know what? We can have some of those tomor-

The television does come on. After a lot of snow, the reception clears to show a news program in black and white. *Black and white!* Miss Ida is adjusting the rabbit-ears antenna sitting on top of the TV (Auntie Dee explained what it was on their first visit to Miss Ida's), but Deja is losing interest. She's seen old TV programs in black and white, and they just don't look right.

"What do you want to see?" Miss Ida asks.

"My favorite show is on Channel Ten."

Miss Ida turns to Channel Ten, but the screen goes all snowy again.

"Looks like we don't get Ten." Miss Ida turns to another channel. "How about some music?" She sits on the couch and pats the place beside her.

Deja is going to be stuck watching Miss Ida's boring old music program on Miss Ida's old black-and-white television. Someone is playing the accordion and two women in funny-looking clothes are singing a song that Deja doesn't even like.

"Everyone loves music," Miss Ida says.

Later, Miss Ida shows Deja the room where she'll sleep. It is small and drafty and has a single bed with a nightstand and a dresser. She shows her

The television does come on. After a lot of snow, the reception clears to show a news program in black and white. *Black and white!* Miss Ida is adjusting the rabbit-ears antenna sitting on top of the TV (Auntie Dee explained what they were on their first visit to Miss Ida's), but Deja is losing interest. She's seen old TV programs in black and white, and they just don't look right.

"What do you want to see?" Miss Ida asks.

"My favorite show is on Channel Ten."

Miss Ida turns to Channel Ten, but the screen goes all snowy.

"Looks like we don't get Ten." Miss Ida turns to another channel. "How about some music?" She sits on the couch and pats the place beside her.

Deja is going to be stuck watching Miss Ida's boring old music program on Miss Ida's old black-and-white television. Someone is playing the accordion and two women in funny-looking clothes are singing a song that Deja doesn't even like.

"Everyone loves music," Miss Ida says.

Later, Miss Ida shows Deja the room where she'll sleep. It is small and drafty and has a single bed with a nightstand and a dresser. She shows her

the bathroom with the tub on legs and the basin with no cabinet or counter. Everything is strange and doesn't feel right. Nothing is the way it is at home. Deja doesn't like being at Miss Ida's.

Tuesday, Wednesday, Thursday, Friday. That's four whole days. It's going to be like being in jail or something.

Auntie calls before bedtime, and Deja has to answer her questions nicely, since Miss Ida is standing right there.

"Are you having fun?"

"Yes, Auntie Dee."

"Are you being good?"

"Yes, Auntie." Auntie Dee asks to speak to Miss Ida, and Deja hands her the telephone.

"Don't you worry about a thing," Miss Ida says. "We're having a ball over here. You can take your time getting back."

Deja's eyes get big hearing that. She remembers Auntie Dee saying she'd be back before Deja knew it. What if she did decide to take her time? How could Deja bear it?

# 6

# A Party, Just Because

"I put most of my turnips on her plate when she wasn't looking," Deja says to Nikki on the way to school on Tuesday.

"Turnips? Who eats turnips? My mom never cooks turnips."

"I bet you all Miss Ida's friends eat turnips."

"Maybe it's something only old people eat."

Deja thinks about this. It sounds right to her.

"Are you going to be at Miss Ida's on your birthday?"

"No! Auntie Dee's coming back on Friday. And my birthday is Saturday. You know that."

Nikki had been with Deja when she picked out her invitations at the stationery store in the mall. She liked that they were in the shape of a big pink birthday cake. She thinks about how much fun it's going to be when she hands them out to each girl in her class, even Antonia. Who will probably be surprised, but Auntie Dee is making her invite *all* the girls. Maybe she should just put the invitations in their cubbies. That way, everyone will be surprised.

Auntie had told her to give them out last week, but she kept forgetting. Anyway, Deja didn't think it mattered all that much. She'd been talking about her upcoming party for weeks.

As soon as they walk through the school gates, they stop. Across the yard, a group of girls are clustered around Antonia. She is handing out small white envelopes to each reaching hand. All the girls from Room Ten, from Mr. Beaumont's class, and from Mrs. Miller's are there.

The first bell rings, and everyone freezes. Beatriz holds her hand in the air in mid-reach. Antonia grins as she holds the white envelope inches from Beatriz's hand. The bell rings again, and everyone bursts into laughter. Antonia hands Beatriz the envelope, then skips to the line where Ms. Shelby is already waiting for the class.

"They're for my party," Antonia whispers to Deja as she passes by. "I was going to invite you,

but I know you're already having your own party."

"What's in those envelopes?" Nikki whispers to Deja as they take their places.

"They're for *her* party," Deja whispers back.

The class marches into the school in line order. At the cubbies, while everyone is getting things out of their backpacks before they put them away, Antonia reaches over Deja and hands one of the small envelopes to Rosario.

Rosario slips an invitation out of the envelope, and she and Deja and Nikki look at it together.

Just Because . . .

Come to my Just Because party on Saturday at 2:00 p.m.
. . .just because.
There's going to be a roller rink, a trampoline, and a tetherball (in the ground).
We're going to decorate our own cupcakes and make our own sundaes.
It's going to be fun, fun, fun and you're invited!
Please come.

Deja stares at the invitation.

"I don't believe it," Nikki says.

"What?" Rosario asks.

Deja reaches into her backpack and pulls out one of her birthday-cake invitations.

"Look."

Rosario opens the invitation and reads it. "Ohhh," she says. She looks at Deja and raises her eyebrows. "What are you going to do?"

"I'm having my birthday party. What do you think?"

Suddenly, they hear Ms. Shelby say, "I'd like all those holding conferences at the cubbies to wrap it up and get to their desks."

They quickly put away their lunches and backpacks, scoot to their desks, and pull out their morning journals. Deja decides to write about Antonia being a copycat. On purpose.

## Tuesday

*The worst Tuesday ever. Antonia is having a party the same day I'm having mine. On purpose. It's called a "Just Because" party and she says she's having it just because but she's really having it to ruin my party. Because she knew I was having one and she probably didn't think that I was going to invite her but Auntie Dee was making me anyway. She's going to have a bunch of fun stuff and now I bet everyone's going to go to hers and not mine.*

Deja thinks of her invitations. They looked so festive just that morning when she put them in her backpack. She remembers thinking about how much fun she was going to have as she bestowed one on each girl in her classroom. Now they seem sad and pathetic.

"Help me put my invitations in the cubbies," Deja tells Nikki after everyone has filed out to recess and Ms. Shelby has dashed out of the classroom to heat up her mug of water for tea. Deja knew this would be the best time, because Ms. Shelby heads to the teachers' lounge to heat a mug of water every recess unless she's holding kids in for not doing their homework. She hands half of the envelopes to Nikki.

After they've put one in each girl's cubby, they walk out onto the yard to survey where things stand. Everything looks normal. Kids jumping, kids running, kids socking balls or kicking them. . . . But nothing's normal. A terrible wrench has been thrown into Deja's big plans.

They settle on a bench to watch some girls from their class jump rope until the freeze bell rings. Nikki knows what Deja is thinking, and Deja knows what Nikki is thinking. Of all those girls, who is going to come to Deja's party now?

# 7

# Nemesissis

After recess, Deja listens to Ms. Shelby going on and on about a field trip that's coming up. How "certain people" might not be able to participate because "certain people" haven't been doing their homework and have been getting into trouble on the yard and are having a hard time staying on task when it's time to work. Deja ticks off each thing. She does her homework, she doesn't get in trouble on the yard, and she generally stays on task. So she's definitely not "certain people."

Deja looks over at Antonia. Unfortunately, Antonia's not "certain people," either. She usually does what she's supposed to do—at least in front of the teacher's face. Now Antonia is sitting with her hands folded, staring at Ms. Shelby. She has a little, serene smile on her face, which makes her look somewhere between happy and satisfied.

Next Ms. Shelby talks about sack lunches and what they can and cannot bring on the field trip. Fruit is good, but sodas are a no-no, as are candy and gum. Also, they are to bring a pad and pencil to the boring natural history museum, because they will be expected to take notes.

Deja's mind drifts to the invitations sitting in the cubbies. Her heart sinks at the thought of them winding up at the bottom of everyone's book bag, forgotten until it is time to clean out backpacks at the end of the school year. She thinks of how carefully she'd filled them out in her best handwriting in purple, because it's close to her favorite color, lavender, and it goes so well with her second favorite color, pink.

After all that trouble, who is going to want to come to *her* party? There is no roller rink planned. No trampoline. No decorate your own cupcake. No make your own sundae. Just a cake and favors and chips and punch and vegetarian pizza and videos and double dutch and games. All she can picture, now, is her and Nikki sitting at the table with party hats on their heads—by themselves.

Miss Ida is in the kitchen cooking dinner when Deja comes in through the side door. Nikki follows close behind. "Hi, Miss Ida," Deja says.

"Hello, Miss Deja," she says, looking up with a smile. "And you brought your little friend, Nikki."

"Hello, Miss Ida," Nikki says.

"Is it okay if Nikki visits a while?" Deja asks.

"Why, sure, sweetie."

Deja nudges Nikki, and they both look at the bubbling pots on the stove. Nikki gives Deja a sympathetic look.

Deja leads the way to the living room. "We can watch TV, but it's in black and white."

"Black and white? Let's go out on the porch," Nikki suggests.

"Offer your little friend a piece of candy," Miss Ida calls from the kitchen.

Nikki's eyes widen, and she immediately looks at the dish of peppermints on the coffee table. She smiles broadly.

Deja can't help but giggle as she holds the dish out to Nikki.

"What's so funny?" Nikki asks, plucking a peppermint from the bowl.

"Nothing."

Nikki pops the candy in her mouth and

tries to suck on it, then begins to chew slowly.

Deja bursts out laughing, watching the look on Nikki's face go from anticipation to confusion. Nikki chews and chews and finally swallows. "What's *wrong* with this candy?"

"It's kind of old." Deja's giggle turns into a laugh. "You should have seen your face! You want another piece?"

"That's not even funny," Nikki says. She wanders over to peer at the old black-and-white photographs on Miss Ida's mantle. There is a picture of a man and a woman standing in front of a barn. The woman is holding a baby in a bonnet. Babies don't wear bonnets anymore.

"That's Miss Ida's mother and father," Deja tells Nikki. "And that baby is Miss Ida."

Nikki's eyes get big. "*That's* Miss Ida?" The baby looks happy and plump. She looks as if she's just getting ready to laugh out loud. Miss Ida is like her baby self, Deja realizes. She is still happy and plump. Her old black-and-white TV and funny telephone are just fine with her. She's never had any kids, and that seems to be just fine as well.

Out on the porch, after Nikki has gone home, Deja's mood changes. Now she feels stuck at Miss Ida's, and no one is going to come to her

party, not even her "far-away" daddy, probably. And she has to worry if Miss Ida is making those nasty beets for dinner.

Deja goes back into the kitchen to watch Miss Ida cook.

"You gonna spoil my surprise," Miss Ida says as Deja sits down at the kitchen table. "I'm making you a before-the-birthday birthday cake. Something to hold you over until you can eat your real birthday cake."

"You're making me a cake?"

"If that's all right with you. We'll have it when it's closer to your birthday."

Deja is quiet for a moment. Then, before she knows it, she blurts, "This girl—at school—she's having a party on the same day as my birthday party."

"Oh? You two have the same birthday?"

"No, Miss Ida. She's having a 'just because' party."

"Well, what on earth is that?" Miss Ida is stirring the cake batter by hand. The fat under her upper arm jiggles with each stroke.

"It's a party just because. That's why she's calling it a 'just because' party."

Miss Ida stops stirring and squints her eyes. "Is this little girl your friend?"

"Not really," Deja says.

"Did she know about your party?"

"Everybody knew. They were just waiting for me to give out the invitations."

"Hmm. Sounds like this girl might be your nemesis."

"What's a *nemesissis?*"

"Nemesis. Kind of like a competitor. Someone who competes with you. Now, there are other meanings—stronger meanings—but I think the one I'm thinking of is the one for you."

"Nemesissis," Deja says.

"No, nem-e-sis," Miss Ida says. "Don't worry. They usually get what they deserve."

# 8

# All This Party Talk

gain, when Deja wakes up the next morning, it takes a minute to realize where she is. Then she remembers. Miss Ida's. She sits up and looks around. It's different from her own bedroom at home. The furniture is dark and heavy. On top of the dresser there's a white lace runner, and more pictures. Someone in a cap and gown, someone leaning against an old-fashioned-looking car with pointy fenders. Someone sitting on a porch, waving at the camera. These are all Miss Ida's people.

I have people, too, Deja thinks. I don't have a mama anymore, since she died and went to heaven, but there is Auntie Dee and my daddy (Auntie's baby brother), and there is Great-Aunt

Minerva, and my granddad Paw Paw (Auntie Dee's daddy), and Uncle Bill and Aunt Mildred. There are cousins, some close to Deja's age, some far from Deja's age. She has plenty of people.

"Plenty of people," Deja says, standing on the bed so she can see most of herself in the mirror.

Miss Ida is stirring oatmeal when Deja enters the kitchen. The birthday cake is hidden. "Well, there you are," Miss Ida says. "Did you sleep well?"

Deja thinks about this. She doesn't know if she slept *well*, because she was asleep when she was sleeping. "I might have slept well, Miss Ida."

"I certainly hope you did, because we got work to do today."

"Work?"

"After school. Wednesday is my dinner-delivery day. I make dinners for the shut-ins."

"What's a shut-in, Miss Ida?"

"Someone who just can't get out. Maybe they're too sick or handicapped or too old. I could use an extra set of hands this day. When you get back here, I'm gonna dish my chili into these Styrofoam containers." She points at the stack of containers and plastic lids on the table. "And you're gonna snap those plastic lids on top."

*Assembly line,* Deja thinks. They'd learned

about that in Social Studies. She remembers how Ms. Shelby had them line up in three groups of eight. Then she gave each team captain a plain piece of cardboard. Everyone had a task to do when the card came to them. Each person had stuff to decorate their team's card. Those cards looked so funny when they reached the end of the line. Glitter, sequins, bits of ribbon, clumps of confetti. Deja liked that. She's looking forward to coming back to Miss Ida's and getting started.

Later, when she heads down the front porch steps to join Nikki for the walk to school, she thinks of what Miss Ida told her: *Nemesissis.* She's got a nemesissis.

"Guess what Antonia is?" Deja says to Nikki as they walk down Fulton Street.

"What?" Nikki asks.

"Miss Ida says she's my nemesissis."

"What's that?"

"Someone who's super jealous of another person."

"Really?" Nikki says.

Deja nods her head, and thinks, *Well, it kind of means that.*

As soon as Deja and Nikki get to school, they discover that the whole class—the girls, at least—is abuzz over Antonia's "just because" party. Ms. Shelby has to squelch excited whispers that keep popping up during Spelling Wizard activities.

Then, during silent reading, a note gets passed to Deja. Each girl has written down her name and what she's planning to wear to the party. It's at just that moment that Ms. Shelby walks over to Deja, plucks the note off her desk, and holds it up to the class. She reads each name and what that person plans to wear, then says, as she tears the paper neatly in half, "If I come across any more of this during class time, the girls in this room will be spending their recess on the bench." She looks around. "All week."

Deja's mouth drops open. She and Nikki look at each other. It would be so unfair to get punished for something they've got nothing to do with. It would be nice to see all the girls get punished for acting silly and disloyal and not even mentioning her invitation, but she doesn't want to be included.

Deja makes a mental note. Every girl in her class is just ignoring her invitation. It's almost as if she hasn't even given them out. Well, if they're not going to say anything, she's not, either. So there.

At late recess it's Nikki's turn to be in charge

of the long rope. Once out on the yard, Nikki and Deja run to their favorite spot under the big tree next to the chainlink fence. It's out of the sun and away from the boys. Half the girls from their class run behind them to line up for jump rope.

"I'll be a turner," Deja announces. "Nikki, get the other end." Deja doesn't want half their recess time taken up with a stupid argument about who is going to turn. The line that forms is long, but she knows she's going to go after Tina, the last girl in line.

*"Mabel, Mabel, set the table and don't forget the red-hot pepper!"*

On "pepper," she and Nikki turn the rope as fast as they can. The game is designed to make it hard for the jumper without pulling the rope. She and Nikki are able to get several jumpers out. It's such fun that she forgets all about Antonia's last-minute copycat party. In fact, she's suddenly sure that all of the girls in Ms. Shelby's class like her much better than Antonia and will choose *her* party after all.

When the second bell rings, she and Nikki run toward the line to help their class be ready to be dismissed to their classroom first. Suddenly, Nikki bends down and picks up something off

the ground. She looks at it and shoves it into her pocket, but not before Deja sees her do it.

"What's that?"

"What?" Nikki says.

"That thing you put in your pocket."

"Nothing."

Deja holds out her hand. "Let me see it, Nikki."

Nikki reaches into her pocket slowly. She pulls out the note and hands it to Deja.

It's a note between Melinda and Rosario. Melinda wrote:

> I can't wait until Saturday and Antonia's party!
> What about you?

Then Rosario had written back:

> I'm going to skate the whole time.
> Beause I know how to turn now.
> I'll teach you how.

It was probably a note they'd been passing back and forth in class. One of them had dropped it on the playground without even noticing. Deja puts it in her own pocket and walks on ahead of Nikki. She has nothing to say.

"Deja, come on," Nikki says, walking fast to catch up.

"See? I told you Antonia was my nemesissis," Deja says.

Nikki returns the jump rope to the ball cabinet and they go to their seats, and then the worst thing happens. There's a small white envelope on Deja's desk. She looks around, wondering who put it there. She opens it up and reads the scribbled note across the top of the invitation:

You and Nikki can come too if you want.

Antonia is inviting them to her "just because" party. Deja frowns and turns to look at Antonia, but Antonia has already taken out her math journal and begun working on the Problem of the Day posted on the white board. Deja looks over at Nikki. Nikki's working on it as well. She feels complete bewilderment. She doesn't know what to think. She reaches into her desk to take out her math journal. She doesn't want Ms. Shelby to think she's one of those "certain people" who has trouble getting on task in a timely fashion.

# 9

# Miss Ida
# Explains the World

They make a good assembly line, Miss Ida says, once they get going with the dishing out and snapping the lids on.

"Miss Ida," Deja says, "that girl I was telling you about—she gave me an invitation to her party."

Miss Ida chuckles. "Oh, little girls, little girls. . . . They learn such cleverness at such an early age."

Deja doesn't know what to make of that. It's been a truly puzzling day. First, no one saying anything about her invitations. And then finding that note on the yard. And getting that invitation from Antonia. She decides to think about something else—something completely different, something she's been wondering and waiting for the right moment to ask about.

"Miss Ida, did you know my Auntie Dee when she was a little girl?" Miss Ida has lived on Fulton Street ever since Deja can remember. Maybe she lived there when Auntie Dee was little, and Deja's daddy was even littler. When Grandma Kate was still alive and before Paw Paw had to move in with Uncle Bill and Aunt Mildred.

"I remember your Auntie Dee when she was a little bitty thing," Miss Ida replies.

Deja finds it hard to imagine Auntie Dee little. Deja wants to ask another thing, but she thinks better of it. She really wants to ask Miss Ida if she thinks her daddy will come to her party, but she keeps her mouth closed. She doesn't know why.

"Now, see, some of these folks have nobody to come visit them and we're the highlight of their week," Miss Ida says as they go up the walkway of the first shut-in. "This shut-in, Mr. Peeples, he doesn't like change. Not at all. It'd be fine with him if things just stayed the same forever."

Deja looks at the shut-in's house. It looks like a house of someone who is shut in. Miss Ida's told her that Mr. Peeples lives all alone, with just a cat and a parrot. His house sits back from the sidewalk and has a long, deep covered porch hidden behind a screen. Miss Ida starts up the walkway, but Deja hangs back. The clapboard front is dark and scary. Also, there is a pile of newspapers covering the front steps. It looks spooky.

Miss Ida reaches back and grabs Deja by the hand. She pulls her along. "Whatcha dawdling for? We can't take all day."

Miss Ida knocks on the shaky screen door, then rattles the handle. "Come on, Mr. Peeples. Open up. You know you love my chili. Come on, don't be ornery."

"No one's being ornery," Mr. Peeples says as he opens the door, then looks down at Deja. "Who you got here?"

"My little neighbor. Now let us in."

Mr. Peeples's living room is dark enough to need a lamp turned on, too, just like Miss Ida's. Deja wonders why old people don't like sunlight. She plans to ask Nikki if she's ever noticed this.

"What did you have for breakfast?" Miss Ida asks. She goes to the buffet in the dining area and pulls open a drawer. She gets out a place mat and a napkin. She opens another drawer and gets out a spoon. She's explained to Deja that Mr. Peeples's wife has passed recently but he keeps everything the same, as if she is going to come home any minute.

Mr. Peeples says nothing. He walks over to the dining room table and takes a seat. Suddenly, a fat orange cat trots into the room and leaps onto the table. It settles down next to the chili Miss Ida has put in a bowl.

*Auntie Dee sure wouldn't allow a cat on the table,* Deja thinks.

"What's your name?" Mr. Peeples asks.

"Deja."

"How old are you, Deja?"

"I'll be eight on Saturday. It's my birthday."

"Aah, you got a birthday comin' up." He smiles and the orange cat yawns. "So what are your plans?"

"I'm having a party, but nobody's coming." *Except maybe my daddy,* she thinks, and it feels like she has a secret.

"Why is no one coming?"

"Because they're going to this other girl's party. This girl named Antonia."

"You mean they're going to skip yours and go to hers?"

"Nobody is even saying anything about my invitation. So I'm not going to say anything, neither."

"Like a standoff," Mr. Peeples says.

Deja doesn't know exactly what that is, but it sounds right. "Yeah, like a standoff," she says.

Mr. Peeples squints his eyes. He looks at Deja for a long moment. "I'm sure someone's going to show up."

The way Mr. Peeples says that, Deja wonders if he's talking about her daddy. But why would he? He doesn't even know her daddy. Nikki will be there, of course. . . . But two's not a party.

The next shut-in is Mrs. Lutz. She lives in a small apartment over the cleaners. She is hard of hearing, so it takes a long time for her to come to the door, too. Miss Ida has to say everything twice because Mrs. Lutz hardly ever wears her hearing aid. She says it whistles. She never knows when it is going to whistle because it does it when it wants to.

"See, now, Mrs. Lutz, she's stubborn, and her stubbornness causes her to make things hard for herself. She could always get that hearing aid fixed," Miss Ida says once they've left the apartment. "Deja, take my advice. Don't develop stubbornness. It makes life difficult."

Deja doesn't think she's stubborn. But then, remembering how she put off cleaning her bedroom, she decides maybe she is, a little bit.

✿

Miss Maple is the last shut-in. She spends a lot of time on her front porch watching the comings and goings of her neighbors. She's the most interesting, with her tidbits about the people who live around her. "I ain't nosy, mind you. I'm concerned. I'm kind of like a neighborhood watch all by myself." She directs Miss Ida to put the chili in the refrigerator. "I'll get to it later, Ida," she says of the chili. "How would you-all like some homemade fudge?"

The three of them sit on the porch swing and watch Miss Maple's street with her. Every once in a while, Miss Maple makes a comment about this neighbor or that. She knows interesting stuff, and Deja could sit on her porch all day. It's actually better than TV—especially when Miss Maple brings out the platter of her homemade fudge.

*Too bad Nikki's not here,* Deja thinks. Fudge is her second-favorite food, after chocolate-chip cookies.

All this visiting shut-ins makes the afternoon go by faster—and the time when Auntie Dee will be returning that much closer. Deja knows that when she wakes up it will be just one more day until Auntie Dee picks her up. Just a little while until she'll see if anyone is coming to her birthday party after all, and . . . if her daddy is coming.

Happily, Miss Ida has prepared something yummy for dinner. As a treat, she sets up the meatloaf, mashed potatoes, and corn on the cob on TV trays in the living room. She turns on the old black-and-white TV, and they watch the news while they eat. Deja looks down at her plate. Not one green vegetable. Auntie Dee would never have prepared such a meal. But isn't it nice to eat like this every once in a while?

One thing about Miss Ida—she loves to talk to the television. A lost dog has walked all the way from campgrounds by a lake to its home. Eighty-three miles, and he knew just how to get there! Miss Ida claps and whistles and says, "You are one smart dog! Yes, you are!"

While Miss Ida goes out to the kitchen to get two slices of the before-the-birthday birthday cake, a man comes on and talks about how they should raise taxes for something. Deja can't figure out what he's saying. "I'd like to see *you* live on a fixed income, mister," Miss Ida says, returning with the cake. Then she lists all the stuff she has to pay for on her fixed income.

Deja takes a big bite, and with a mouthful of yummy cake she asks, "What's a fixed income?"

"It's money you have to live on. And it stays the same amount, no matter what."

Deja still doesn't understand it, but she knows it isn't anything she has to understand, yet. She looks over at Miss Ida. It hasn't been *so* bad spending the past three days with her. It had seemed like a long time at first. Now it seems like just a short time has passed.

After she brushes her teeth and says her prayers, she climbs into bed and lies there a long time, thinking. She plans to ask Auntie Dee straight out if her daddy is coming for her birthday or not. She wonders what Auntie Dee will say. She wonders if Auntie Dee even knows.

Deja also decides that the next time Auntie Dee has to go out of town and she can't stay at Nikki's, she'd like to come back and stay with Miss Ida. For one thing, she makes really good before-the-birthday birthday cake. Deja had two big pieces.

# 10

# Life Back to Normal—Kind of

Deja sits on her own porch, waiting for the cab that will bring Auntie Dee home. She's glad it's Friday after school. She's glad she doesn't have to hear everybody whispering about Antonia's party anymore. Rosario and Melinda had the nerve to walk up to her at recess and ask her if she was coming to Antonia's party. She turned around and walked the other way.

Nikki, beside her, is busy writing in her notebook. "What's that?" Deja asks finally.

"I'm listing all the stuff we can do at your birthday party tomorrow."

"It's only going to be the two of us, Nikki."

"Well, we can still have some fun."

"No, we can't. Everything is ruined." Deja

sighs. "All I want is for it to hurry up and be over."

Nikki continues her writing, and Deja continues watching the corner, waiting for the cab to turn onto their street. When it does—slowly driving down Fulton—Deja jumps up and does a little dance. *Auntie Dee is back!*

"Auntie Dee!" Deja runs crashing into her arms before she can even pay the driver.

"My goodness, Deja. I haven't been gone that long."

"It seemed like forever."

Deja grabs Auntie's bag by one handle and Nikki grabs the other. They walk with her into the house.

"Ready for the big day tomorrow?" Auntie Dee asks. Deja shrugs, but Auntie seems not to notice. She pulls back the drapes to let some sunlight into the darkened living room. Deja smiles. It is good to get back to sunny rooms.

After Nikki's mom calls her home for dinner and Auntie Dee has come back from Miss Ida's to thank her and offer her some payment (which Miss Ida refuses), Auntie orders pizza to celebrate being home. "So you think no one is coming tomorrow?" she asks Deja. When Auntie Dee had called the night before, Deja told her about the no RSVPs and how everyone was going to Antonia's and how Antonia had even asked her, Deja, to her party. "Don't worry," she'd said to Deja. "I'll see what I can do."

They're sitting at the coffee table, eating off paper plates. Deja loves when they eat pizza this way. It's more fun than sitting at the table in the kitchen.

"Antonia's party is going to be better."

"Well," Auntie Dee says. She looks as if she is thinking—hard. "Maybe a small party will be better than you think. Maybe," she adds, as if she has something in mind. Deja looks at Auntie Dee carefully. Is she thinking about Deja's daddy coming? Is this the time to bring him up? They hardly ever talk about him. Auntie Dee always seems to change the subject when Deja mentions him. Deja knows she has to be careful.

Deja takes a deep breath. "Auntie Dee?"

"Yes, sweetheart?"

"Do you think my daddy will show up for my birthday, since he didn't make it last year? Or the year before that?"

Auntie doesn't answer right away. She stops eating and sighs. "Deja, I sent your daddy an invitation, but I haven't heard anything. I'm sorry, baby. Maybe he didn't get it. Perhaps where I sent it isn't his current address."

Auntie Dee looks down, and Deja knows that Auntie doesn't believe that. What she believes is that her daddy *isn't* coming. "I'm thinking we won't see him," Auntie Dee says finally. "I'm sorry."

She looks at Deja closely, but Deja looks away. She doesn't know what Auntie Dee wants her to say. So he's not coming *this* year. Then he'll probably come next year. Yes. That will be better, actually. She doesn't want her daddy to see that she had a party and nobody came. "That's okay, Auntie Dee. He'll probably come for my ninth birthday. I can wait."

In the moment of quiet that follows, Deja thinks about how far into the future next year seems. It's going to take so long to get to be nine.

Later, after they've eaten the pizza and Deja has helped Auntie Dee unpack, Auntie Dee makes a few telephone calls to the mothers she knows from PTA. As she sits at the kitchen table talking, Deja sits on the couch combing her Barbie's hair and listening. It's so hard when things don't go the way you've been imagining them. So far,

nothing is the way she thought it would be just five days ago.

Now she hears: "Oh, yes. I see. No, no, I understand. Okay, maybe next time." It doesn't sound very good, not very promising. After she hangs up, she dials another number. Deja hears a better conversation from Auntie Dee's end. "Oh, great. Good. I'll see you tomorrow. Yes, at two."

Auntie Dee hangs up and calls out, "Well, Sheila Sharpe is coming, after all."

*Sheila Sharpe!* Deja thinks. *Sheila Sharpe, who breathes through her mouth? That's who's coming to my party?* Now she pictures herself and Nikki . . . and Sheila Sharpe . . . sitting at the dining room table in party hats. Not good.

"Well," Auntie Dee says from the doorway. She claps her hands once. "It seems no one got your invitations, and they've already committed to going to the other party."

"Nikki and me put the invitations in everyone's cubbies."

"Could they have fallen out?"

"No. Someone must have taken them out!"

"Now, don't go accusing someone if you don't know for sure."

"I bet you Antonia saw us."

Auntie smiled cheerfully. "I'm going to make

a couple more phone calls tonight, and the rest in the morning. We'll have some kind of party yet."

Deja doesn't want "some kind" of party. She wants the party she's been imagining for the last three weeks.

Deja doesn't like the look on Auntie Dee's face when Deja pads into the kitchen the next morning, still in her nightgown. Auntie Dee breaks into a big smile as soon as she sees her, but Deja knows it is a forced smile. "There's the birthday girl," Auntie Dee says cheerfully over her newspaper. She gets up and gives Deja a big birthday hug. "Happy birthday, big girl. I got something for you."

Deja sits down and puts her chin in her hand. Auntie pushes a small box toward her. *A small box means jewelry,* Deja thinks. Deja stares, making no move to open it. She just wants to look at the box wrapped in lavender tissue paper for a while first. Finally, she removes the paper, lifts the top off, and peers inside. It's a citrine pendant on a gold chain.

"It matches my ring," she says softly.

"Do you want to put it on?" Auntie asks.

"Okay."

Auntie Dee slips the necklace around Deja's

neck and then fastens the clasp. "Beautiful," Auntie says.

Deja rubs the citrine, liking the feeling under her fingertips. Then she goes to the mirror over the buffet in the dining room. She has to jump up to get a really good look at it in the mirror. She likes what she sees. "Thank you, Auntie Dee," she says, coming back into the kitchen.

"Look what else I have for you," Auntie Dee says. On the table is Deja's favorite breakfast, the one she never ever gets to have—except on her birthday. On Auntie Dee's best china plate is a single cinnamon bun, like the kind they sell at the mall. Gooey and dripping with icing. Deja can never eat a whole one, but she always thinks she can when she starts. She peels off a piece and licks the icing. She licks all the icing clinging to her fingers. She feels a little better.

"Now, Deja, I made some calls last night and some this morning. It seems most of the girls in your class are going to Antonia's party, but a few are now undecided. There's nothing we can do about it, so let's think of something fun you, me, Nikki, and your little friend Sheila can do."

Deja sits up straight at the mention of Sheila Sharpe. *She's not my friend!* she wants to say. But she doesn't. She realizes fully what a dud her party is going to be and slumps her shoulders. She looks out the kitchen window at a cloud-covered morning. The wind rattles the leaves on Auntie Dee's maple trees. Even the day is disappointing. Where is the sun?

# 11

# A Turn of Events

The party will start at two—with hardly any guests, unless some of the "undecideds" decide to come.

Nikki pops over with lavender and pink streamers. "Look, Deja. I've got your favorite colors."

"Great."

"Come on, Deja. Some girls might come. Don't you want the living room to look pretty? I brought lavender and pink balloons, too."

Deja shrugs. "I guess." She holds out her hand, and Nikki gives her a package of lavender streamers.

Working alongside Auntie Dee, they hang paper streamers in the living room. Then they set up the card tables with the board games and bring out the big stuffed panda bear that will be first prize. On each table, they place bowls of popcorn and peanuts. Deja had already made sure nobody had any peanut allergies back when she thought the entire classroom of girls was coming. Then they start blowing up the balloons. Auntie Dee has even set up an empty card table in the corner for birthday presents. Deja looks over at the nearly empty table. So far there's only Nikki's present. She supposes that soon there will be at least one more . . . from *Sheila Sharpe*.

In the refrigerator sits Deja's lavender birthday cake with the pink flowers. In the freezer is Deja's strawberry ice cream, because pink and lavender make such a happy combination, and Deja, with her decorator's eye, knows this.

Just then, Deja, Nikki, and Auntie Dee hear a loud cracking sound. They stop as if the freeze bell has rung in the living room. Deja waits to see what will follow. Silence. And then another louder cracking sound. Deja and Nikki rush to the living room window just as a steady downpour begins.

"It's raining," they say in hushed tones. They slap palms, but in a way that shows they barely believe it. It's *raining*. Great big drops pelt the sidewalk, Auntie Dee's tiny white compact car in the driveway, Mr. Bohanna's lilac bushes. It's *raining*. On Deja's birthday.

But that means it's also raining on Antonia's backyard. It's raining on her trampoline, on her roller rink, and on her tetherball (built into the ground). On her party that's supposed to take place—now! Nikki and Deja look at each other as a slow smile grows on each of their faces. Nikki starts the song first. Soon Deja joins her, until they are skipping around the living room hand in hand:

*It's raining, it's pouring,*
*The old man is snoring.*
*He bumped his head and went to bed*
*And couldn't get up in the morning.*

"Again!" Deja demands, so they sing it again.

*It's raining, it's pouring,*
*The old man is snoring.*
*He bumped his head and went to bed*
*And couldn't get up in the morning.*

"Again!" Deja says louder. And they sing it again. And again, and again, until Auntie Dee says, "Okay, enough." Then they just skip around the room humming.

Sheila Sharpe soon arrives. Deja opens the door just as Sheila's pushing her glasses up on her nose with her index finger. The first thing she says as she hands Deja a big box wrapped in the funnies from the Sunday paper is, "Sorry, we didn't have any wrapping paper."

"That's okay," Deja says. "Thanks." She puts the big box on the table next to Nikki's much smaller flat box wrapped in silver paper and a lavender ribbon. Deja guesses Nikki's gift might be a coffee-table book of beautiful houses for her future decorating business. She'd pointed it out to Nikki the last time Auntie Dee had taken them to the bookstore.

"This is exactly what I want for my birthday," she remembers saying while running her hand over the book's slick cover.

Nikki, Deja, and Sheila go out to the front porch to watch the rain. Even Bear—poor nearly forgotten Bear—seems to be watching the rain from his post on the porch swing.

"Can we swing on that?" Sheila asks.

"Our legs aren't long enough yet," Nikki explains.

"I'll push," Deja says.

Nikki and Sheila climb on, and Deja begins to push the swing while the rain comes down harder and harder.

After a while, Auntie Dee sticks her head out the door to say, "Well, it looks like your little friends Ayanna and Rosario are heading this way. I just spoke to their mothers on the telephone."

"You think they're bringing presents?" Nikki says.

Deja shrugs. At this point, she doesn't know what to think. Nothing is as she'd imagined. It's not as good as she'd imagined it would be three weeks ago . . . but it's not as awful as she'd imagined it would be last night. Even with her daddy not coming. Like Auntie said, she probably didn't send the invitation to the right address. That's the reason. Next year they'll find out his correct address and send an invitation there. Then of course he'll come. He's her daddy.

The telephone rings again. And again. A few minutes later Auntie Dee's back announcing, "Three more, it seems. Melinda, ChiChi, and Keisha."

Deja counts. Eight all together. Enough for two games.

By two thirty, there are enough girls in Deja's living room to occupy all of the card tables. Excited, giggly voices fill the room. Deja, at the Monopoly table, with Park Place *and* Boardwalk, looks around. Almost all the girls from Room Ten are there. Deja is finally eight, like most of her classmates. Only Nikki and Rosario are still seven. What a satisfying feeling. Deja throws the dice and lands on Community Chest.

It's funny how one thought leads to another thought. Deja thinks of being eight. She thinks of how powerful and strong the number "eight" sounds, while "seven" sounds soft and babyish. "Eight" makes her think of a figure eight on ice. And that makes her think of skating, which makes her think of roller rinks, which leads her to Antonia's roller rink under the pounding rain. And Antonia sitting at her kitchen window, staring at it.

She reads the card. *Get out of jail free.* She sighs heavily. Not because of what it says—that should make her smile—but because she knows what she's going to do. She's going to sit there and feel *sorry* for *Antonia.* And she's not going to have all that much fun if she feels sorry for Antonia. She sets the card down and watches Keisha throw the dice. She tries to put Antonia out of her mind. But Antonia keeps popping back into it. Does this mean what she thinks it means?

"Yes. It does," she says under her breath, and the girls at her table glance up.

But Antonia took Deja's invitations out of the cubbies.

Deja frowns. Then she thinks, *It could have been Carlos or Ralph who took the invitations out of the cubbies.*

Now she's feeling even sorrier for Antonia. When Auntie Dee stops by the table to replenish the potato chip bowl, Deja beckons for her to lean down. She whispers her idea in Auntie's ear, and Auntie breaks into a big smile. "I knew you'd want to do that," she says. "I knew you'd start to feel sorry for Antonia and want to invite her."

"You did?" Deja asks.

"You're my Deja, aren't you?"

Deja feels a surprising warmth wash over her. She likes the way Auntie Dee says "my Deja."

She watches Keisha move her wheelbarrow five spaces and land right on Park Place. Ha! Deja holds out her hand while Keisha counts

Monopoly money into it. *This feels great,* Deja thinks. She places the money into the right piles and looks at it. She's probably going to win. She loves winning. But she doesn't love it more than hearing Auntie Dee say "my Deja."

"My Deja" tells her that even though she doesn't have her daddy—this year—she has her Auntie Dee. And, to Auntie Dee, she is "my Deja."

Plus, there's always next year to hope for.